J+

W9-BZW-000

GOOF−OFF
GOALIE

GYM SHORTS

GOOF-OFF GOALIE

Betty Hicks

Illustrated by Adam McCauley

ROARING BROOK PRESS

NEW YORK

Many thanks to Gary Anderson, youth soccer coach,
for his helpful suggestions.

Text copyright © 2008 by Betty Hicks
Illustrations copyright © 2008 by Adam McCauley
Published by Roaring Brook Press
Roaring Brook Press is a division of
Holtzbrinck Publishing Holdings Limited Partnership
175 Fifth Avenue, New York, New York 10010
www.roaringbrookpress.com

Library of Congress Cataloging-in-Publication Data
Hicks, Betty.
Goof-off goalie / Betty Hicks ; illustrated by Adam McCauley. — 1st ed.
p. cm. — (Gym shorts)
Summary: Ten-year-old Goose is best at goofing off, but when he decides to become
the goalie for their soccer team, his friend Henry sets up a practice schedule and
enlists their other friends to help Goose improve his skills.
ISBN-13: 978-1-59643-244-4   ISBN-10: 1-59643-244-6
[1. Soccer—Fiction. 2. Friendship—Fiction. 3. Determination (Personality trait)—
Fiction.] I. McCauley, Adam, ill.   II. Title.
PZ7.H53155Goo 2008   [Fic]—dc22   2007015223

Book design by Jennifer Browne
Printed in the United States of America
First edition June 2008
2   4   6   8   10   9   7   5   3   1

For Quinn

CONTENTS

A WIZARD?

Goose made the wish on his birthday.

He closed his eyes. He blew out ten candles. And he wished that Alex Winkler would vanish.

One week later, Alex did.

Vanish.

Just like that. Poof.

He was gone.

Alex and his whole family packed up and moved to Vermont.

Goose was excited. Because that meant Alex couldn't be the goalie on Goose's soccer team anymore.

Goose wanted to be goalie.

He loved being on a soccer

team, but he hated all that running. Goalies didn't run as much. They got to stand still a lot. And dive into the dirt.

But Goose felt guilty. He had made something strange happen. After all, Alex was in Vermont.

Goose asked his friend Henry, "Do you think I might be a wizard?"

Henry sat on Goose's front steps, rolling a soccer ball from one foot to the other. "No," said Henry. "Why?"

"Because I wished Alex Winkler gone."

"You did?"

"Yeah. I wished it on my birthday cake."

"That was awesome cake."

"Yeah."

Goose pictured his birthday cake. Chocolate with Tootsie Pops stuck all over it. Goose loved Tootsie Pops.

He pulled an orange one out of his pocket and popped it into his mouth.

"On *my* birthday," said Henry, "I wished I was the greatest soccer player on earth."

Goose grinned his famous goofball grin. "Didn't come true, did it?"

"No," said Henry. "But next year *you* can wish that I'm the greatest soccer player on earth. Then, if it happens, we'll know you're a wizard."

"You're crazy," said Goose. "I'm not wasting my wish on you." He swirled the Tootsie Pop on his tongue.

"Do you think coach will let me be the new goalie?"

Henry didn't answer. He seemed to be thinking.

Goose flung his arms wide open. "Look at me," he exclaimed. "I'm tall. My arms are long. I can fill up more goal space than anybody."

Henry still didn't say anything.

"And," Goose added, "I would never get bummed if guys blamed me for losing. You know me." Goose blew a giant spit bubble. Then he stuck the Tootsie Pop back in his mouth. "I don't *care* what people think."

Henry nodded. He picked up the soccer ball and held it. "I don't think Coach will go for it."

Goose blipped the Tootsie Pop out of his mouth. "Why not?"

"You goof off," said Henry.

"I do not!" cried Goose.

"Coach thinks so," said Henry. "He says you don't focus."

"I do too," Goose argued. But he knew it was true. Sometimes he spaced out. He didn't mean to. It just happened.

"Besides," said Henry, "you've never even played goalie."

"But I can," said Goose. "I know I can. I watched the World Cup on TV. All the moves. I can do them."

"Yeah? Show me." Henry kicked the ball straight at Goose.

Goose dove for it. He landed in a boxwood bush. He
never touched the ball.

"Goose?" said Henry.

"What?"

"You need a better plan."

HOT STUFF

The next day, Goose arrived at soccer practice early. He went straight to Coach's office. He stuck his head in the door. "Coach?"

"Yeah?" Coach raised his head from the papers he was grading.

"Can I ask you something?"

"Sure," said Coach.

Goose stood in the doorway. He pulled on each of his fingers. He jerked his head one way. Then he jerked it the other way.

"Is anything wrong?" asked Coach.

"No," said Goose. He twitched one shoulder.

Goose wanted to be the new goalie, but he didn't know how to ask. He couldn't just say, "Can I be the new goalie?" That might sound like he thought he was hot stuff.

Coach hated kids who thought they were hot stuff.

"Can I be the new goalie?" Goose blurted.

Man. He'd blown it already.

Coach raised his eyebrows. The look on his face said, *Goalie? You? Are you kidding me?*

But all Coach said was, "Well . . . Goose. You know Marcus is our back-up goalie. He already knows how to play the position." Coach rubbed the back of his neck. "Of course," he added, "you're welcome to try out."

"Great!" shouted Goose.

Coach shifted in his chair. "Uh, Goose . . ."

"Yes, sir?"

"It's hard to play goalie."

"Yes, sir. I know."

"You have to be quick."

"I'm quick." Goose nodded eagerly.

"You can't blame yourself for losses," said Coach.

"I never blame myself," said Goose.

Coach laughed. Then his face got serious again. "Goose," he said, "you have to focus."

"I focus."

Coach looked at him. He started to say something. But he stopped. He rubbed his neck some more. Then he pushed his chair back from his desk. He stood up and said, "Sure, Goose, let's see what you can do."

Goose ran all the way to the field. It was the fastest he'd ever run in his whole life.

Coach got there a week later. Maybe it was only three minutes. But it seemed like a week.

Goose stood in front of the goal. Feet apart. Arms out. Ready for anything.

Coach kicked the ball to his left.

Goose dove for it. He stretched his body straight out into the air—just like he'd seen the pros do.

He landed face-first. His mouth full of dirt.

The ball landed in the back of the net.

Goose touched his front teeth to see if they were still there. They were.

He wiped blood off his chin. He spit out a pebble.

"No, Goose, no," said Coach. "You were too close to the goal. Move out. Widen the angle. Are you okay?"

"Yeah," said Goose. But he didn't feel okay. He felt stupider than dance lessons. Half his team had arrived for practice. They were all watching.

"I'll say one thing," said Coach. He shook his head and laughed softly. "You've got guts."

"Thanks!" said Goose. He hopped to his feet.

"But you don't have to knock all your teeth out. There are safer ways to land, you know."

Goose didn't know.

"And easier ways to stop most shots," said Coach. He walked over and patted Goose on the back. As if he were a puppy. A puppy that could never learn anything. One that would pee on the rug forever.

Goose sneaked a look at his teammates. Most of them were laughing.

Goose smiled his famous goofball grin.

Because he didn't know what else to do.

Besides, he didn't care what they thought.

He'd show them.

THE WRONG WISH

Coach made everyone jog around the track that looped the soccer field. Five times.

Goose thought racehorses should run around tracks. Not people.

But he had no choice.

So Goose ran until he wanted to barf. Three laps. No way could he do five. He had to stop.

Goose bent over and gasped for breath.

"Goose!" warned Coach.

Goose's friend Henry jogged by. "You can do it," he urged.

Goose started running again.

He ran. And ran.

Until he got a stitch in his side. It felt as if he'd fallen on a steak knife. It hurt like crazy. But he finished.

Next, everyone did hamstring stretches. Goose bent over and grabbed one ankle with both hands. He counted to ten. Then he did the same motion with the other ankle.

Goose liked stretching. He got to rest while it looked like he was doing something.

After warm-ups, Coach divided everybody into two teams.

Goose played sweeper. Marcus played goalie. Henry played striker.

Henry dribbled the ball all the way down the field.

Rocky scored off a volley shot from Henry.

Henry and Rocky were good. So good they kept the

ball at the other end of the field forever. Nothing happened where Goose was. He was the last player with a chance to stop the ball before it reached the goalie.

To pass the time, he blew spit bubbles. Goose could blow monster spit bubbles. But he didn't want to goof off. So he only blew a few.

Next, he thought about how good a Tootsie Pop would taste. He thought about the new video game he'd gotten for his birthday. He thought about how his socks had slipped too low over his shin guards.

He bent over to pull them up.

"Goose!" shouted Marcus.

Goose jerked up. Too late.

A player zipped past. He angled a chip shot over Marcus's head and into the net.

Coach shook his head at Goose. Then shouted, "Wake up!"

Goose wished he had moved to Vermont with Alex Winkler.

But, wait! Marcus wasn't so great. He hadn't stopped the ball either.

Coach trotted over to Marcus. "Nice try," he said. "When the ball's that high, push off with one foot when you jump. You'll go higher."

Then he walked over to Goose. "If you'd been paying attention, Marcus wouldn't have moved too far from the net."

Oh, thought Goose. "Sorry."

"That's enough play for now," said Coach. "Who wants to try out for goalie?"

Marcus and Goose raised their hands.

Coach waited for more hands to go up.

None did.

"Fine," said Coach. He rubbed his neck again. "Marcus, you and Goose stay here. Practice keeping the ball out of the goal. The rest of you guys line up and work on passing drills."

Yes! thought Goose. I can do this.

Goose took the first turn as goalie.

Marcus kicked low balls to him.

He kicked high balls to him.

He kicked balls straight into Goose's body.

Goose caught two balls. Coach didn't see either save.

Instead, Coach saw every ball that Goose missed. All two million of them.

I'm such a moron, thought Goose. Why did I wish Alex Winkler gone? Why didn't I just wish to *be* the stupid goalie?

He subtracted six from the number of days in a year. That left 359 days until his eleventh birthday.

No way.

Goose needed to make a new wish, *now*!

SOCCER EVERY SECOND

When Goose arrived home after practice, Henry and Rocky waited at the top of his driveway.

They lived on the same street.

Their friends, Rita and Jazz, lived there, too. It was awesome to have five friends so close together. They had exactly enough people for a basketball team.

"Look!" yelled Rocky. He waved a book in the air. The cover said *Improve Your Goalie Skills.*

"I don't need a book," said Goose. "I need a wish. Plus talent. And a new brain."

"Come on," said Henry. "You just need a plan."

"Do I look like a man with a plan?" said Goose.

17

He felt heavy. As if his shoulders were sinking into his elbows.

Henry and Rocky slapped Goose across the back. "*We,*" said Henry, "are about to turn you into the greatest goalie on earth."

"Yeah?" asked Goose. "How?"

"Practice," said Rocky.

"Lots of it," said Henry.

"Every day," they said together.

"We'll use my backyard goal," explained Henry.

Anything to do with sports, Henry owned it. Balls, bats, goals, hockey pucks. It wouldn't surprise Goose if Henry had a golf course.

Henry was a sports nut.

So Goose walked to Henry's house with Henry and Rocky. Rocky's bulldog, Chops, trotted behind them.

Rocky sat on the grass and read aloud from his goalie book. Chops sprawled beside him. Chops had sad eyes. Even when his tail wagged.

"*To catch a ground shot,*" read Rocky, "*point your fingers down and spread them out.*"

Henry kicked a ground shot to Goose. Goose

spread his fingers and dove in front of it. His funny bone hit the ground. Hard.

A million tiny bombs exploded up his elbow. "Aaagh!" Goose groaned. *What sicko had named it a funny bone?*

"Don't dive at every ball!" shouted Rocky.

Goose wiped blood off his elbow and said, "I like to dive."

"Fine," said Rocky. He flipped to another page. *"When diving for the ball,"* he read, *"the caught ball should hit the ground first. This will cushion your fall."*

"What if I don't catch it?" Goose asked.

Rocky flipped more pages. He shrugged. "I guess you'll just bleed a lot."

"Gee, thanks," said Goose. Maybe he *should* learn other ways to stop the ball.

Rocky helped the first day. After that, it was Henry who was always there.

Soccer every second—Goose knew it was Henry's idea of heaven. Each day for two weeks, Henry helped Goose practice drills from Rocky's book.

He kicked balls to Goose. To the right. To the left. Ground shots, high shots, body shots. From every angle.

When Henry went inside to eat supper, Goose kicked the ball by himself. He threw it. He rolled it.

When Henry came outside after dinner, Goose headed the ball. Sometimes he dove for it. He learned to land without breaking his arm.

One day, it rained. Goose stayed home.

Henry called him on the phone. "You won't melt. Get over here."

Goose went.

Every day, Goose wished he'd made a smarter wish. Or that he had a magic wand.

Then he could cast a spell. And turn himself into a goalie. *Zap*! Overnight.

Practicing was hard. Every day with Henry. Plus regular practices, twice a week.

Goose had played his new video game only one time. He didn't even have time to blow a spit bubble. And his dinner was so late, it felt like breakfast.

But his parents let him. As long as he did his homework.

"We're proud of your effort," they said.

Effort was the parent word for, "Yay! You're not goofing off."

Each night, Goose slid into bed like a noodle.

Two minutes later, *buzzz*! His alarm went off.

The clock always said that nine hours had passed.

Ha!

The clock lied.

Goose would drag his body out of bed anyway. All his muscles ached. He felt like a giant toothache. He didn't care.

He was improving.

Meanwhile, Marcus owned the goalie spot.

Goose didn't blame Coach. After all, Marcus was better.

Just one more week, thought Goose. Maybe two. He'd be ready. Not the greatest goalie on earth. But good enough.

Even Henry was impressed. He joked with him and said, "Who *are* you?"

Goose grinned his goofball grin. "Not Goose," he said. "Somebody else."

The next day, Goose showed up at Henry's house. Henry looked sadder than Rocky's dog.

Something was wrong.

A Problem

"We have a problem," said Henry. He slumped against a tree.

"What's wrong?" asked Goose.

Henry looked weird. Was he sick? Would he be able to help Goose practice?

"My grades," moaned Henry. "They're awful."

"Man," said Goose. "That's too bad."

Goose was relieved. Henry's rotten grades had nothing to do with him. Did they? But why had Henry said, "*We* have a problem"?

"My parents went nuts," said Henry. "They said I spend too much time on sports."

"No way," said Goose. "You're on just one team. Remember the time you played baseball, swam, *and* ran track?"

"Yeah," said Henry. "But that was summer. No homework. No school."

"So, what's up with them?" asked Goose. "They wouldn't make you quit soccer, would they?"

"Not yet," said Henry.

Goose felt relieved again. The soccer team would be toast without Henry.

"I can't help you practice anymore," Henry whispered.

"What!"

"I can't help you—"

"I heard you. I heard you. No way. That's not fair. They can't do that. I need you."

"I know," said Henry. "I'm sorry."

Henry hung his head. He traced tiny circles in the grass with his toe.

"What will I do?" asked Goose. "I'll never be goalie without help."

Henry raised his head. "Don't worry." He forced a smile. "I have a plan."

"Yeah?" Goose looked hopeful. "What?"

"Here." Henry shoved a folded piece of white paper at Goose.

Paper? What kind of help was paper?

BRING BAND-AIDS

Goose reached for the piece of paper Henry handed him.

Henry couldn't help Goose practice anymore. How could paper help?

Goose unfolded it and read:

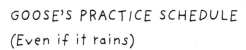

GOOSE'S PRACTICE SCHEDULE
(Even if it rains)

Monday: Rita

    Saves—

        1. Ground shots

        2. High shots

        3. Body shots

Tuesday: Jazz
  Throwing—
        1. Rolling the ball
        2. Shoulder throw
        3. Overarm throw

Wednesday: Rocky
  More saves—
        1. Punching the ball
        2. Tuck and slide
        3. Dives (go easy)
        Bring Band-Aids

Thursday: Rita
  Kicking—
        1. Goal kick
        2. Volley
        3. Half volley

Friday: Rocky
  Extra drills—
  Work on biggest problems

Saturday: Rita, Jazz, Rocky
    Scrimmage

Sunday:
    Start over (See Monday)

"Wow!" cried Goose. "You did this? You arranged this? Rita, Jazz, Rocky? They'll all help me?"

"Yeah." Henry's mouth smiled, but his eyes showed no signs of life.

"Henry," said Goose. "What's wrong?"

"Nothing," said Henry. "I'm glad I helped."

"Thanks, man!" Goose tried to high-five Henry. But it was like slapping hands with a dead guy. Why wasn't he happy? He'd fixed the problem!

Maybe Goose should bring Henry a waffle. Henry loved waffles.

"Henry," said Goose. "Look at this." He waved the paper in the air. "It's neat. It's detailed. If this were homework, you'd get an A."

"Yeah." Henry laughed a sour laugh. "I've got to go inside now."

"Sure," said Goose. "See you later. But, Henry . . . thanks!"

Henry was already at his back door.

"Hey!" called Goose.

Henry turned.

"Can I use your goal?"

"Sure," said Henry. Then he vanished inside his house.

SCABS

Monday:

Rita and Goose moved Henry's soccer goal to Goose's yard.

Rita always walked as if she were dancing. And dressed up girly. It was hard to think of her carrying a soccer goal, but she did.

Rita was tough. And tall. *And*, she played goalie.

"Your fingers are too close together," she said. "Keep your eye on
the ball," she said. "Relax your body."

"Stop!" said Goose. "One thing at
a time."

But Rita's help was huge. Goose
learned so much, he offered her his
last Tootsie Pop.

It had melted some. But the paper
stuck in only two places.

"Yuck," said Rita.

Tuesday:

Jazz was small, but quick. She
showed Goose how to get rid of the
ball fast. Before the other team had
time to regroup.

"I can't move that fast," said
Goose.

"Sure you can," said Jazz. "Focus."

"Easy for you to say," said Goose.

Wednesday:

"If you dive to save every ball, I'll go home," said Rocky.

"It's my skin," answered Goose.

"You don't have much left," said Rocky. Goose's arms had more scabs than skin.

"Whatever," Goose grumbled.

Just to make Rocky happy, Goose practiced punching the ball away.

Thursday:

It rained so hard, the goal had puddles in it.

"No practice today," said Rita.

"But Henry said—"

"Do I look like Henry?" said Rita. She jammed her fists on her hips. "Really, Goose. Give it a rest. You've earned it."

Goose offered her a whole bag of Tootsie Pops. Fresh ones. As soon as he had money.

Friday:

Makeup day with Rita. Goose hoped Henry wouldn't care that they were off schedule.

Saturday:

Rita, Jazz, and Rocky fired a million shots at Goose. Like bullets. Goose stopped all but three. He got rid of each ball. Fast.

"You're ready!" shouted Jazz.

"Yahoo!" screamed Rita.

"We're out of Band-Aids," said Rocky.

Sunday:

Goose took the day off. He hoped Henry wouldn't mind. After all, he was ready!

Monday:

Goose had a *real* game. With his soccer team. Coach put him in at sweeper. Once. Most of the game, Goose sat on the bench.

He blew so many spit bubbles, he could've made it into the *Guinness World Records* book.

"Please, Coach," said Goose. "Let me play goalie. I'm good now. Honest. I've practiced a billion extra

hours. Look at how many scabs I've got."

"Friday." Coach smiled. "You'll get your chance."

"Really?" said Goose. "Friday?" Goose thought maybe he hadn't heard right.

"Marcus will be out of town. You're it," said Coach. "Don't be late."

A BETTER REASON

Goose hadn't thought about Henry in over a week. He'd been too busy. And too excited. He was going to play goalie! On Friday!

Rita, Rocky, and Jazz restarted Henry's practice schedule. Drills, saves, kicks, throws. Every day.

The day before the game, Henry stopped Goose in the hall at school. "You ready?" asked Henry.

"Totally!" said Goose.

"Nervous?" asked Henry.

"No," Goose lied. He had the jitters so bad, he couldn't even eat.

"I hated missing your practices," said Henry. "It killed me."

"Really?" said Goose.

"Yeah," answered Henry.

Wow, thought Goose. Was that why Henry had

acted so bummed? Because he didn't get to help me?

"Are your grades better?" Goose asked. Until right this second, he had forgotten that Henry even had grades.

"No," said Henry. "And if they get any worse, I have to quit soccer."

"No way!" Goose exclaimed.

"Yeah." Henry hit a locker with his fist.

All through English, Goose worried about Henry.

Give up soccer! Henry lived for soccer. Or baseball. Or whatever. Henry had to have sports. He'd die. Didn't his parents know anything?

Goose's teacher, Ms. Mann, switched to math. Goose switched to worrying about tomorrow. Friday. The day he would get his chance. One chance.

He couldn't blow it.

What if he got sick? What if he got chicken pox?

He felt fine now, but who knew?

What if his mom had a car wreck driving him to the game?

No. The game was near school. He'd walk.

What if he got hit by a truck?

It could happen.

What if he was late? Coach had a rule. Kids who were late didn't play. No excuses.

Goose laughed. What was the matter with him? I mean, come on. He wouldn't get sick. Or hit by a truck. And he would *not* be late.

He'd spend the night on the soccer field. Or skip school. *No way* would he be late.

"Don't forget," Ms. Mann instructed the class. "Book reports are due tomorrow. Also, read chapters

BOOK
REPORTS
DUE
TOMORROW

ten and eleven in your history books. We're starting a new unit on—"

Tomorrow! Goose tuned his teacher out. He couldn't think about English, or history.

Tomorrow was his chance.

Goose thought back. Why had he wanted to play goalie? So he wouldn't have to run as much. That seemed dumb now. It also seemed like years ago.

I've got to be goalie, thought Goose. For just one reason. Because I love it.

Would he play great?

Or would he stink?

HELPING HENRY

Friday. At last.

Goose hadn't slept since Wednesday. He was too excited. And nervous.

He didn't hear a word Ms. Mann said all morning.

"Relax," Henry told him at lunch. "You'll play great."

Goose hoped so.

Henry shoved his lunch tray aside. He pulled a green folder out of his book bag. "My book report," he said proudly. "I worked on this for two weeks."

"No kidding?" Goose had spent two minutes on his. "Think you'll get an A?"

"Yeah," said Henry. "I do. Honest. It's the best thing I've ever done."

"Cool," said Goose. "Now your parents can ease up."

"Yeah," said Henry. He leaned closer. "But, Goose," he whispered. "I need your help. I didn't have time to read my history chapters. I'll get a zero."

"You want me to zap history into your head?" asked Goose. "Since I might be a wizard?"

"No," said Henry, rolling his eyes. "I'm going to the school nurse after lunch. I feel barfy."

Goose slid away from Henry. He didn't want to get sick.

"No," said Henry. "I'm not really sick. I just need to miss history. Then I'll be well again."

"Oh," said Goose. He slid back.

"But I'll miss English, too. Would you give Ms. Mann my book report?"

"Sure," said Goose.

After lunch, Goose sat in class wishing *he'd* gone to the school nurse. His chicken sandwich had morphed back into real chickens. All pecking and clucking in his stomach.

Goose thought three o'clock would never come.

Finally. The bell rang.

Goose bolted for the soccer field. He arrived early. Dressed. Ready to play. Feeling like the best goalie on earth.

Coach wasn't even there yet. Or Rocky. Or Henry.

Goose was glad Henry was about to get his grades fixed. His book report—

Henry's book report!

Goose never turned in Henry's book report!

He looked at his watch.

Did he have time to walk back to school? *And* find Ms. Mann?

It was three fifteen. The game started at four. But players had to be there thirty minutes early. At three thirty. Or they couldn't play.

The walk took ten minutes. Twenty minutes both ways. Add five extra minutes to find Ms. Mann.

Goose did the math. Forty-five minus thirty equaled fifteen minutes. Minus twenty. Henry hated

word problems. Minus another five. Equaled—not enough time.

What if he ran?

Goose hated running. He'd never make it.

He couldn't risk it. If he were late, his team wouldn't have a goalie.

But if Henry got a zero on his book report, he'd have to quit soccer. Their team would lose its best scorer.

Goose might lose his best friend.

But . . . but. Geez! Goose had worked for weeks!

So had Henry.

Goose sank onto the nearest bench. He covered his face with his hands.

STEAK KNIVES

Goose started running.

He knew he'd never make it.

So . . . why try?

Goose didn't know. All he knew was that he was running.

And that he'd never be goalie.

He had wasted two whole minutes thinking. Now he had thirteen left. *If* his math was right.

Who knew? Who cared? *Just run*.

Goose found Ms. Mann in the teacher's lounge.

"What! Goose. You're not allowed in—"

"No time," said Goose, gasping. He shoved the green folder into Ms. Mann's hands. "It's Henry's."

He sucked in breath. "I had it in class. Honest. On time. My fault."

Goose turned and bolted out the door.

He'd never run so fast in his life. Ow! Major stitch in his side. Killing him. Not like one steak knife. More like ten steak knives.

Can't breathe. Got to stop. Can't stop.

What time is it? Watch is blurry. Three thirty? No! Please. Not yet. Eyes sweaty. Can't see.

Soccer field ahead. Team huddled around Coach. Too late.

Goose collapsed in a heap at Coach's feet.

"Goose!" exclaimed Coach. "What the—"

"Wh . . . wh . . ." Goose's tongue wouldn't work. He licked his dry lips and swallowed. "What t-time is it?" he asked, gasping.

Coach looked at his watch. "Three thirty."

Goose had made it!

FOCUS!

Goose sat on the bench beside Henry. Sucking in air. Trying to get his breath back. Waiting for the game to start.

He felt as if he'd won a solid gold trophy. But he hadn't won anything. Yet.

He still had to play. He had to stop goals.

"You okay?" asked Henry.

"Yeah."

"Did you give Ms. Mann my book report?"

"Yeah."

"Any problems?"

"Nope."

Henry nudged Goose with his elbow and said, "Thanks."

"You're welcome." Goose meant it.

"The nurse knew I was faking," said Henry. "From now on, I'm doing *all* my homework."

Thweet! A whistle signaled the game was about to start.

Goose stood in front of the goalie box. Not too close. Not too far out. Ready. Pumped.

Focus, he told himself. The other team has on blue. Don't take your eyes off them.

For fifteen minutes, Rocky and Henry kept the ball at the other end of the field. Their offense was awesome. But no one scored.

Goose worried. He needed action.

He thought about his amazing run to school and back. Ha! Maybe he should try out for track. He tried to blow a spit bubble. His mouth was too dry.

"Focus!" he hissed.

All of a sudden, blue shirts were everywhere.

Surrounded by the yellow shirts on Goose's team. A blue-shirt player broke free. He dribbled toward Goose. He kicked the ball.

It flew straight at Goose. He relaxed his body. He let the ball sink back into his stomach. Then he wrapped his arms around it. He'd caught it!

Goose ran forward. Quickly. He drop-kicked the ball downfield.

Coach gave him a thumbs-up.

Goose's insides cheered like crazy. Wait! Blue shirts. They were back!

Goose moved out from the goal. Too far? He hoped not. The ball soared over his head. *And* over the crossbar. Out of play.

Whew!

By halftime, Goose had made five saves. All of them easy.

"Good job," Coach told him. Coach turned to Goose's teammates. "Great offense. You kept their goalie too busy to breathe. But guys! We haven't scored. We need a goal!"

One minute into the second half, a missed shot hit the post and flew toward Henry. He headed it into the net. Score!

Goose cheered.

A minute later, Goose was surrounded again. Blue shirts and yellow shirts. So many bodies. So many feet. *Where was the ball?*

Then he saw it. Spinning through the air toward the far side of the goal. Out of his reach.

Goose pushed off with the foot nearest the ball. He dove. He stretched his arms toward the ball. He caught it!

Goose let the ball hit the ground first. He brought his knees up and wrapped his body around it. He didn't even bleed.

Goose was so pumped up he thought he might burst.

Focused? Yes, he was focused! He'd never been so focused in his life.

The ball. Blue shirts. Yellow shirts. They were all he could see. All he could think about.

Here they came again.

No problem. Goose was in control.

Their striker was wide open. Dribbling toward the left corner of the goal. Goose moved over to cover the shot.

But the striker passed the ball. To the right. An open forward kicked it into the net. Score!

Goose felt stupid. Like an idiot. Why hadn't he stayed in the middle? The score was tied. It was his fault.

"It's okay," shouted Coach. "Shake it off."

No time to think about it.

Goose stayed busy. He had six more saves. After each one, he rolled the ball. Or he threw it. Or he kicked it away. Quickly. To a teammate.

With three minutes to play, Rocky chipped the ball over the other goalie's head. Into the net. Yes!

The score was 2 to 1. Goose's team was winning.

Three more minutes, Goose told himself. Focus.

His team was playing good defense. They kept the ball away from his goal.

Time *must* be running out. Suddenly, a player on the other team took one last shot. From way out.

Goose saw it coming. Soaring. High. Should he dive to block it? Or jump? Could he reach it? He didn't know.

The ball was so high. Headed into the upper left

corner of the goal. It could drop in over Goose's head.

He jumped. His arms stretched up. He knew he couldn't catch it. With his finger tips, Goose pushed the ball up and over the crossbar. Safe!

Thweet!

They had won!

A NEW WISH

Goose relaxed in a booth at the Waffle House. His friends surrounded him. Henry, Rocky, Jazz, and Rita.

Goose's parents were so proud. They'd given him money to treat his friends. Goose picked the Waffle House because Henry loved waffles.

"You were awesome!" said Rocky.

Goose shrugged and said, "Thanks." Like it was no big deal.

Who was he kidding?

It was the biggest deal on earth. He was the new goalie! Coach had said so. Well . . . he said Goose and Marcus would take turns. That was fine. For now.

But someday, Goose wanted to be the best goalie on earth. He would never stop practicing.

Goose dug deep into his pants pocket and pulled out five birthday candles. He stuck them into his waffle.

"Whose birthday?" asked Henry.

"Nobody's," said Goose. "But this is a celebration. Why not make a wish?"

"It has to be cake," said Rocky.

"Says who?" said Goose. "I want to make a wish and find out if I'm a wizard."

"Yeah," said Henry. "He's going to wish that I'll be the best soccer player on earth."

"Yeah, right," said Goose.

"He's going to wish *he'll* be the best soccer player on earth," said Jazz.

Goose motioned for the waitress to bring matches.

"One candle for each of us," said Goose. "Everybody makes a wish. Everybody blows them out."

"You're making stuff up," said Rocky. "It won't work."

"It will if I'm a wizard," said Goose.

"I'm wishing for good grades," said Henry. "Then I can play fifty sports."

"Don't say your wish!" Jazz exclaimed. "It won't come true."

The waitress lit the candles.

"Don't anybody spit on the waffle," said Rita.

Everybody closed their eyes. Goose wished that his friends' wishes would all come true. It was the least he could do.